FiZZY

in the Spotlight

FiZZY

in the Spotlight

Michael Coleman

Illustrated by
Philippe Dupasquier

ORCHARD BOOKS

ORCHARD BOOKS
96 Leonard Street, London EC2A 4RH
Orchard Books Australia
14 Mars Road, Lane Cove, NSW 2066
First published in Great Britain 1997
First paperback publication 1998
Text © Michael Coleman 1997
Illustrations © Philippe Dupasquier 1997
The right of Michael Coleman to be identified as the Author
and Philippe Dupasquier as the Illustrator of this Work
has been asserted by them in accordance with the
Copyright, Designs and Patents Act, 1988.
A CIP catalogue record for this book is
available from the British Library.
1 85213 992 7 (hardback)
1 86039 639 9 (paperback)
Printed in Great Britain.

CONTENTS

1

Creepy-crawly!

Fizzy was late.

Not terribly, terribly late, but late enough – and for the third time that week! Her teacher, Mrs Grimm, was already taking the register.

"Alice Frost?"

"Here, Mrs Grimm," called a pretty girl near the window.

Fizzy groaned. Soon Mrs Grimm would reach the Is and be calling for her – Fiona Izzard. Suddenly she had an idea. Perhaps

she could get to her place without being seen.

Squeezing open the classroom door, Fizzy dropped on to her hands and knees. Then, as Mrs Grimm looked down at her register, Fizzy scuttled in through the door and straight under the Nature Table.

She peeped out. Brilliant! Nobody had noticed her. Now what?

At the front, Mrs Grimm called the next

name from her register: "Jason Fry?"

"Here, Mrs Grimm," said a boy at the back.

'Only one more name and it's me,' thought Fizzy. Carefully, she crept out from beneath the Nature Table, making sure she didn't jog it. They were studying insects that week and Jason Fry had brought his spider collection in to show everyone. There'd be no hiding from Mrs Grimm if she knocked that lot on the floor!

As Mrs Grimm looked down at her register

once more, Fizzy took her chance. Darting out from her hiding place she shot beneath a desk. But whose?

Fizzy knew at once. Who wore shoes so shiny you could see your face in them? Who even put their long shoelaces in the washing machine? Who else but the next name on Mrs Grimm's list?

"Lucy Hardwick?" called Mrs Grimm.

It was time to move. Fizzy's name would be called next. She tried to squeeze past Lucy's leg – but, instead, she brushed against it just as Lucy was answering.

"Here, Mrs...aaaaaagghhh!"

"Lucy!" said Mrs Grimm. "What is the matter, dear?"

As Lucy took a quick look under her desk, Fizzy closed her eyes. She was for it now. Lucy would tell on her, just like she always did.

But, amazingly, this time she didn't.

"Nothing, Mrs Grimm," squeaked Lucy. "I just thought I saw a creepy-crawly under my desk."

Fizzy peered up at Lucy Hardwick. "Thanks, Lucy," she whispered as Mrs Grimm turned back to her register. "You're a pal. A creepy-crawly! That was quick thinking."

Lucy simply smiled. "Ah, but do you know what I do with creepy-crawlies?" she said nastily. "I tread on them."

And, with that, she lifted one of her shiny shoes and pressed it down hard on Fizzy's hand just as Mrs Grimm looked up from her register and called, "Fiona Izzard?"

Underneath Lucy's desk, Fizzy bit her tongue. If she screamed, Mrs Grimm would know she was there. But if she didn't scream, Mrs Grimm would think she was absent!

"Maya Sharma," said Mrs Grimm, "have you seen Fiona?"

Fizzy's best friend shook her head. "No, Mrs Grimm."

"I think *I've* seen her," said Lucy Hardwick, pressing her foot down even harder on Fizzy's hand.

"Well, if she doesn't get here soon she'll miss my exciting news!" said Mrs Grimm.

"Exciting news?" said Lucy, sitting up straight.

"Yes," said Mrs Grimm. "The Millington Dramatic Society are looking for a number of schoolchildren to take part in their pantomime this year, and you have all been invited to go along to the Millington Theatre on Saturday for the auditions!"

"Oooh," squeaked Lucy, forgetting about squashing Fizzy's hand. "Is there a starring role?"

"Only one," said Mrs Grimm.

"Is it for a good singer?" cried Lucy.

Beneath the desk, Fizzy was rubbing her hand back to life. Lucy seemed to have forgotten about her, thank goodness. So maybe she could get her own back...

As Lucy went on, "Because I'm a good singer, Mrs Grimm!" Fizzy set to work.

By the time Mrs Grimm said, "I know you

are, dear," Fizzy had almost finished.

And as Lucy asked, "Can I come out to the front and sing a song for everybody now?" Fizzy was done.

Lucy Hardwick swung her legs out into the aisle. She took two steps forward. And then, as she tripped over the shoelaces Fizzy had tied together, she dived headlong against the Nature Table!

"Waaaahhhhh!" yelled Lucy.

"My spiders!" shouted Jason Fry. "She's letting my spiders escape!"

"Waa-aaaa-aahhhhh!" yelled Lucy as Jason's biggest, hairiest spider leapt out of its jar and scuttled down her leg.

While Mrs Grimm was capturing spiders and calming Lucy, Fizzy was able to creep out from beneath Lucy's desk to sit quietly in her place.

"Now, where was I?" panted Mrs Grimm, when she finally returned to taking the register. "Oh, yes. Fiona Izzard?"

"Here, Mrs Grimm!" cried Fizzy. "And I'll be at the auditions on Saturday!"

2

A Bit of a Tail

"What pantomime do you think they're doing?" asked Maya as she and Fizzy set off for the Millington Theatre on Saturday morning.

"*Cinderella*, maybe?" said Fizzy. "Hey, that could be why Mrs Grimm thinks there's a role for Lucy. She's got her down as the Ugly Sister!"

Maya giggled. "There are *two* ugly sisters in *Cinderella*."

"So, Lucy could play both of them," laughed Fizzy. "She's twice as ugly as anybody else!"

The two friends walked cheerfully along the road, kicking up the leaves as they went. They were in good time.

'No chance of me being late today,' thought Fizzy. She bent down and picked up a thin branch which the previous night's strong wind had snapped from a tree.

"Maybe they're doing *Peter Pan*," said Fizzy, waving the branch like a sword. "Now, I could *definitely* play Peter Pan."

"Can you fly?" asked Maya.

"Of course I can't," snorted Fizzy. She swished the branch from side to side. "But I can sword-fight! Peter Pan has that sword fight with Captain Hook, remember?"

They'd reached the small market which was set up in Millington Square every Saturday morning. Millington Theatre was on the other side of the Square. There were stalls all around them.

"On guard!" cried Fizzy, holding out her pretend sword.

"Be careful, Fizzy," said Maya. "You nearly knocked the top off a plant on that stall."

But Fizzy was enjoying herself. "Take

that!" she jabbed. "And that!"

"Fizzy," said Maya anxiously, "I think you should stop."

"Peter Pan doesn't stop until he's beaten Hook, Maya!" shouted Fizzy.

With a dramatic thrust, Fizzy aimed her stick at a beautifully arranged display of bananas on a fruit stall. "Ha-ha! Take that, Hook, you big banana!"

"Ohh, Fizzy!"

Without realising it, Fizzy had jabbed a little too close. "Hello," said Fizzy as she pulled her stick out and found a fat yellow banana on the end, "where did this come from?"

"From there," said Maya, pointing at the banana pile.

"Phew!" sighed Fizzy. "Good job it wasn't one of the bottom ones. The whole lot could have fallen down!"

"Fizzy," said Maya uncertainly, "I think it *was* one of the bottom ones."

Maya was right. The banana Fizzy had just speared *had* been at the bottom of the pile.

Slowly, the pile began to slide…faster and faster until, suddenly, there seemed to be bananas everywhere.

"Oh, no!" groaned Maya. "Now what do we do?"

A deep, angry voice answered her question. It was the deep, angry voice of the stallholder, who'd spent ages setting his display up.

"What you do now," he growled, "is pick them all up again. And you're going nowhere until you do!"

"I think we're late, Fizzy," said Maya as they finally bounded up the theatre steps and in through the swing doors.

Maya was right – again.

"You two are late!" roared Mrs Grimm.

"Sorry," began Fizzy. "We had a bit of banana trouble." She went to show Mrs Grimm her stick, with a banana still jammed on the end, but her teacher cut her short.

"Get changed at once!" shouted Mrs Grimm.

Children were coming down the corridor, dressed in urchin's clothes.

"The changing room is that way," Mrs Grimm pointed. "Now go!"

Fizzy and Maya scuttled off. Reaching the changing-room door, they went inside. There was only one person there, just finishing off her hair.

"Late again," said Lucy Hardwick nastily. "All behind, just like a cow's tail."

"Ho-ho," said Fizzy. "Tell me an udder one, Lucy!"

"Come on, Fizzy," said Maya. "Lucy, what do we have to do?"

"First you have to get undressed," said Lucy. She posed to show off the frilly outfit

she was wearing. "And then you put on some of these theatre clothes."

"Where do we get them from?" asked Maya, as she and Fizzy quickly slipped out of their jeans and jumpers.

"I don't know if I want to tell you ..." began Lucy. Then, as she spotted a small door in the corner of the changing room, she smiled a great big smile. "But I will. You get them from in there."

"Thanks, Lucy," said Fizzy, opening the door.

She and Maya went in. The room was small and dark, with just one little window. They could hardly see a thing.

"Are you sure this is the right place, Lucy?" called Fizzy.

"Oh, yes!" laughed Lucy. And before Fizzy or Maya could do anything about it, she'd slammed the door shut and locked it.

Fizzy hammered on the door. "Hey! Let us out!"

"I will," trilled Lucy Hardwick. "Later! Byeee!"

3

Grrrrrrrr!!

"Now what are we going to do?" asked Maya.

Fizzy didn't know the answer to that one. The room was a bit like the two of them - almost bare! The only other thing in it was a large box.

"I think we'll have to stay here until the auditions are over," said Maya.

"And lose our chance of being in the pantomime?" said Fizzy. "Not likely!"

Fizzy looked around. Aha! She pushed the large box across the floor, so that it was beneath the window. Then, hopping on to the box, she reached up and undid the window latch. Outside was an alleyway, filled with rubbish and old dustbins, and there was a dustbin right beneath where they were.

"Ta-raa!" cried Fizzy. "We can't get out of the door, right?"

"Right," nodded Maya.

"So ..." began Fizzy.

Maya had a sinking feeling. Whenever Fizzy said "So..." trouble wasn't usually far behind.

"So," said Fizzy, "all we have to do is climb out of this window, hop down to the ground and then run round to the front of the theatre and come in again!"

Maya shook her head. "Haven't you forgotten something? We haven't got any clothes to put on!"

Fizzy looked around the little room. Maya was right, of course. There was nothing to be seen. Then she noticed the box she was standing on. So...maybe there was something they couldn't see!

Hopping down from the box, she lifted the lid. There was something inside.

"There you go, Maya, you could wear this." Fizzy had found a black cloak, with a furry collar. It even had a large gold chain to go with it.

"What about you?" asked Maya.

Fizzy had another feel inside the box. There was something else there. And this didn't just have a furry collar - it felt furry all over!

"I can wear this," said Fizzy, pulling out what she'd found.

"But...but..."

Maya stared at the costume Fizzy had in her hands. It had two arms...and two legs...and one tail!

"Fizzy, that's a cat's costume," said Maya. "You can't go out in the street wearing a cat's costume."

But Fizzy was already climbing into it.

"Of course I can, Maya," laughed Fizzy. "Haven't you ever heard of a fur coat!"

* * *

Maya went first.

Hopping out of the window and down into the alleyway, she stood looking up at Fizzy. "Can you get down on your own?" called Maya.

"Of course I can, Maya," laughed Fizzy. "I'm a cat, remember!"

Lifting her furry legs over the windowsill and making sure that her tail didn't get caught on anything, Fizzy hopped down to the ground.

"There you go. Easy! Now all we've got to do is go round to the front of the theatre and in again. We'll be on that stage before Mrs Grimm knows it."

Grrrrrrr!

Fizzy looked at Maya. "I think you'll have to sing better than that, Maya! Even Lucy Hardwick sounds better than that!"

Maya frowned. "Better than what?"

"Better than that growling noise you just made."

"But...I didn't," said Maya.

Grrrrrrr!

"There you go again!" cried Fizzy.

"That wasn't me!" Maya looked at Fizzy. "That was you - wasn't it?"

"It wasn't me," said Fizzy. Suddenly, she had a nasty feeling. "But if it wasn't me and it wasn't you, who was it?"

Grrrrrrrrrr-rrrr!

"It was that!" yelled Maya.

Down at the end of the alleyway was a huge, snarling dog.

"Stay still, Maya," hissed Fizzy. "That's what you have to do. Then it won't chase after us."

"I don't think it wants to chase after *us*," said Maya. "I think it wants to chase after *you*."

"Me?" said Fizzy. In horror, she looked down at her furry arms, her furry legs and her furry tail. "You mean – it thinks I'm a real cat?"

Grrrrrrrrrr-rrrrrrrrrrrrrrrrrrrrrrrrrrrr!

"Yes," said Maya.

"Then forget standing still," yelled Fizzy as the dog started bounding down the alley towards them. "Run for it!"

Down the alleyway they raced.

"It's getting closer!" shouted Maya. "Oh, I wish we'd stayed inside where we were safe!"

Inside? Fizzy skidded to a halt. Just above another dustbin was another window. And it was open.

"Hup, Maya!" yelled Fizzy. "We're going back inside!"

Maya clambered up on to the dustbin, with Fizzy close behind.

Grrrrrrrrrrrrrrrrrrrrrrrrrrrrrrrrrrrrrrrrr-rrrrrrrr!

They were just in time. As the snarling dog leapt for Fizzy's tail, the two friends dived through the open window.

"Phew!" said Maya.

"You can say that again, Maya," gasped Fizzy. "I think this cat's only got eight of her nine lives left!"

They sat up and looked around.

"I wonder where we are?" said Maya.

"In trouble," said an angry voice, "that's where you are!"

4

Fizzy in the Dark

Over in the corner of the room, unloading money from an open safe, stood the owner of the angry voice. And he looked angry, too!

"Who are you?" he snapped.

"My name's Maya," answered Maya. She pointed down at Fizzy, who was still on her hands and knees. "And this is Fizzy."

"Funny name for a cat," growled the man.

"Are you Mr Jenkins, then?" said Maya. A sign with the name "A. Jenkins" was on the office desk.

Fizzy looked up at her friend. Her important-looking black cloak seemed to have made Maya sound important too!

"Er...yes," said the man. "Yes, I am."

"Are you the theatre manager or something?" asked Maya.

"I...er...yes," said the man. "Yes, that's right."

"Good," said Maya. "In that case you'll be able to tell us where the stage is."

"The stage?"

"Yes," said Maya. "We're lost."

"The stage," said the man slowly. "Er...yes. Out of here, turn left, turn right, turn right again and...er...it's straight ahead."

Maya looked pleased. "Thank you very much. Now, let me see if I've got that. Turn left, turn–"

Fizzy couldn't stand it any more. As the man looked on open-mouthed, she leapt to

her feet. "I can remember, Maya!"

"Are you sure?" said Maya.

"Of course I'm sure," said Fizzy, hustling her out of the office. "You know what they say – cats never forget!"

Turning left, Fizzy led the way down a corridor.

"I thought it was elephants who never forgot," said Maya, following her.

Fizzy stopped suddenly. "It is. I've forgotten what he said! Which way now?"

"Right, right again, then straight ahead," said Maya.

They turned right, into another corridor. Then right again, to find themselves at the top of a short flight of stairs.

"He didn't say anything about stairs, did he?" asked Maya.

"No, he didn't. But look!" Fizzy pointed. At the bottom of the stairs was a door. "Straight ahead. That must be it."

The door led into a dark and enormous room, like a big cave. It was full of dusty boxes and bits of scenery.

"I think that Mr Jenkins told us the wrong way," said Maya.

"He said he was theatre manager, didn't he?" said Fizzy. "So this must be the way. Come on, Maya. Maybe there's another door at the end."

Fizzy started to squeeze her way past the clutter. She'd got about halfway when, suddenly, a burst of music began – and somebody started singing.

"It's Lucy!" cried Fizzy. "I'd know that squawk anywhere. We must be close, Maya."

Maya looked up at the ceiling. "But why does she sound as if she's above us?"

"I don't know," cried Fizzy. "Because she's singing high notes, I suppose." Maya was right, though. Lucy did sound as if she was standing right over their heads.

"That Mr Jenkins must have sent us the wrong way," said Maya. "We're not near the stage – we're *underneath* it!"

"Oh, no," groaned Fizzy. "Come on, Maya. We'll have to go back the way we came."

Squeezing her way past a large pillar, Fizzy began to head for the door they had come in by. Suddenly, she found she couldn't move. Something seemed to be holding her back. She tugged and tugged, but still couldn't move.

"Hurry up, Fizzy," said Maya. "We're late enough as it is."

"I can't," said Fizzy.

"Of course you can."

"I can't," wailed Fizzy, "because my tail's caught!"

Behind her, the tail of Fizzy's cat costume was stuck fast between a large handle and the pillar she'd tried to squeeze by. The more Fizzy tugged and the more Maya pulled, the more stuck it became.

"I can't move it," said Maya.

Fizzy saw the answer at once. "Maya, my tail's stuck behind a handle. We've tried to move my tail and we can't. So…"

Maya groaned. "So?"

"So,we move the handle instead!"

"Move the handle? Are you sure? What if something goes wrong?"

"Maya," said Fizzy. "It's just a diddy handle. What could possibly go wrong? Go on, pull it!"

So Maya pulled the handle...and Fizzy found out what could possibly go wrong.

With a mighty whoosh, she shot up into the air and straight through the ceiling!

5

Cat-apulted!

Fizzy felt as if she'd gone somewhere in a very fast lift. But where? Where was she?

Why were there so many bright lights?

Why was Lucy Hardwick sitting on the floor and bawling her head off?

Why were the rest of her class all dressed up and looking at her in a funny way?

Why was Mrs Grimm staring at her with her mouth open? And who was the lady with a clipboard standing next to her?

Suddenly, Fizzy saw what must have happened. The handle Maya had pulled must have been the handle that worked the thingy that shoots actors up on to the stage in a cloud of smoke - and she must have been standing on the thingy! She'd been shot up on to the stage, knocked Lucy Hardwick

flying and messed up everything that was going on!

There was only one question Fizzy couldn't answer. If she had messed everything up, why wasn't Mrs Grimm shouting at her like she usually did?

And then she realised. She was on her hands and knees, dressed in a cat's outfit...

So...Mrs Grimm couldn't tell it was her!

So...perhaps if she pretended to be a real cat, she'd be able to make a dash for it without Mrs Grimm being any the wiser!

So...

"Miaaoww," went Fizzy.

She scampered one way.

She licked her paws and rubbed them across her face.

She scampered back the other way.

"Miaaoww," went Fizzy again.

She even scampered across to Mrs Grimm and rubbed against her leg. With a beam, Mrs Grimm bent down and scratched Fizzy's ear.

It wasn't a big scratch, but it was enough. Her cat's head moved slightly and a bunch of Fizzy's red hair slipped out.

"That isn't a cat," screeched Lucy Hardwick at once. "Cats don't have red hair! Fiona Izzards have red hair!"

"Fiona Izzard?" growled Mrs Grimm.

Fizzy didn't wait for the rest. Still on all fours, she began to race round the stage, dodging in between the other children.

Mrs Grimm gave chase. "Fiona Izzard!" she bawled. "Stop still at once!"

But Fizzy didn't feel like stopping. Round and round she raced, looking for a way out.

"I'll catch her, Mrs Grimm!" shouted Lucy. As Fizzy went past, Lucy dived for her leg, but Fizzy was too quick. Instead, Lucy grabbed Mrs Grimm's leg.

"Ohhhhhh!" cried Mrs Grimm.

"Waaaahhh!" yelled Lucy, as Mrs Grimm fell back and flattened her.

In the commotion, Fizzy saw a set of steps at the side of the stage. Down them she raced ...straight out of a door marked 'Exit'...and straight into Mr Jenkins, the man they'd met in the theatre manager's office!

As Fizzy sent him flying, the bag he was carrying split open. Suddenly it was raining ten pound notes. Oh, she was really in trouble now!

"I'm sorry, Mr Jenkins, Mr Manager, sir," said Fizzy, scrambling around picking up the notes in her paws. "Please don't throw me out of your theatre—"

"Jenkins? Theatre manager?" It was the lady with the clipboard. "I'm Anne Jenkins! I'm the theatre manager!"

Fizzy looked at the man on the floor. "Then who's he?"

"He's a burglar, Fizzy!" It was Maya, rushing down the corridor towards them. "He can't be the theatre manager! He didn't even know the way to his own stage!"

"Well done, Fizzy," said Anne Jenkins after the burglar had been taken away. "But for you, all last night's theatre takings would have been stolen."

"Yes, well done, Fiona," smiled Mrs Grimm. "It looks as if everything's turned out well in the end."

Fizzy laughed. "You mean it wasn't a catastrophe?"

"Far from it," said Anne Jenkins. "It has been a successful morning all round." She turned to Fizzy's teacher. "I would like use your whole class in our pantomime, Mrs Grimm."

As everybody squealed with joy, the theatre manager went on, "And I've also decided who I'd like for the starring role I mentioned."

"Who, me?" piped up a battered-looking Lucy Hardwick.

Anne Jenkins shook her head. "No, there'll be a nice spot in the back row for you, Lucy. The one I want –" she turned to Fizzy – "is you."

Fizzy couldn't believe her ears. "Me? What, as Peter Pan?"

"Peter Pan?" said Anne Jenkins. "Whatever gave you that idea? Our pantomime isn't going to be *Peter Pan*. It's going to be *Dick*

Whittington. And after seeing your performance on stage, I know you'll be just brilliant as Dick's cat!"

As everybody cheered, Fizzy's face split into an enormous smile.

"You look like the cat that's got the cream," whined Lucy Hardwick.

Fizzy laughed. "Can you blame me, Lucy? It has been a purr-fect day!"

Here are some other Orchard books you might enjoy…

TROUBLE FOR DEELA

1 86039 006 4

MUDDLE TROUBLE

1 86039 190 7

SCHOOL TROUBLE

1 86039 179 6

DOUBLE TROUBLE

1 86039 178 8

TREE TROUBLE

1 86039 271 7

CHICKEN MISSION

1 86039 270 9